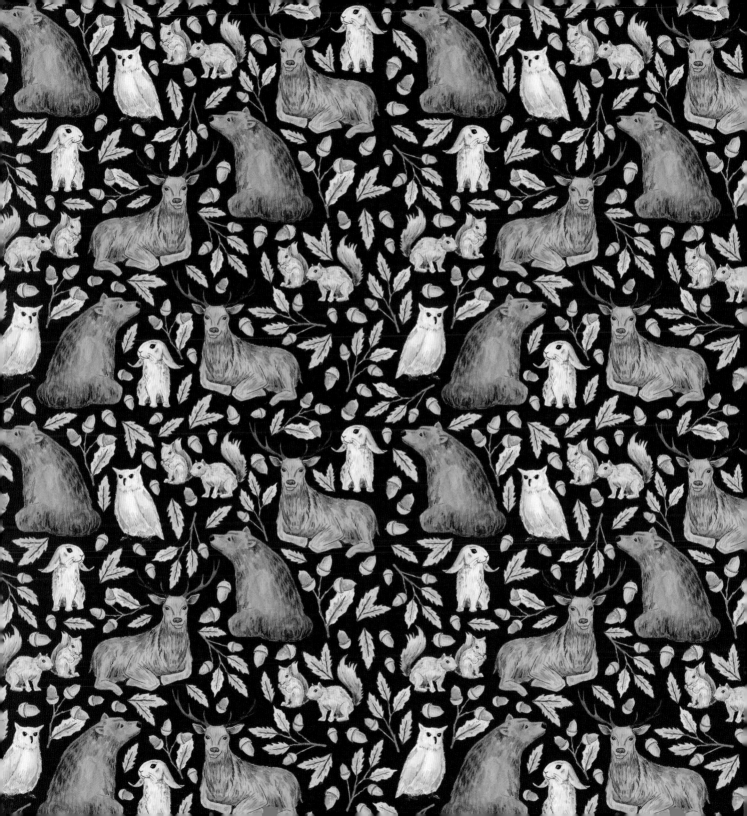

For you, Daddy

Printed in China through AuthorPreneur Central.
First Edition
Hardback ISBN: 978-1-7359901-0-1
Paperback ISBN: 978-1-7359901-1-8

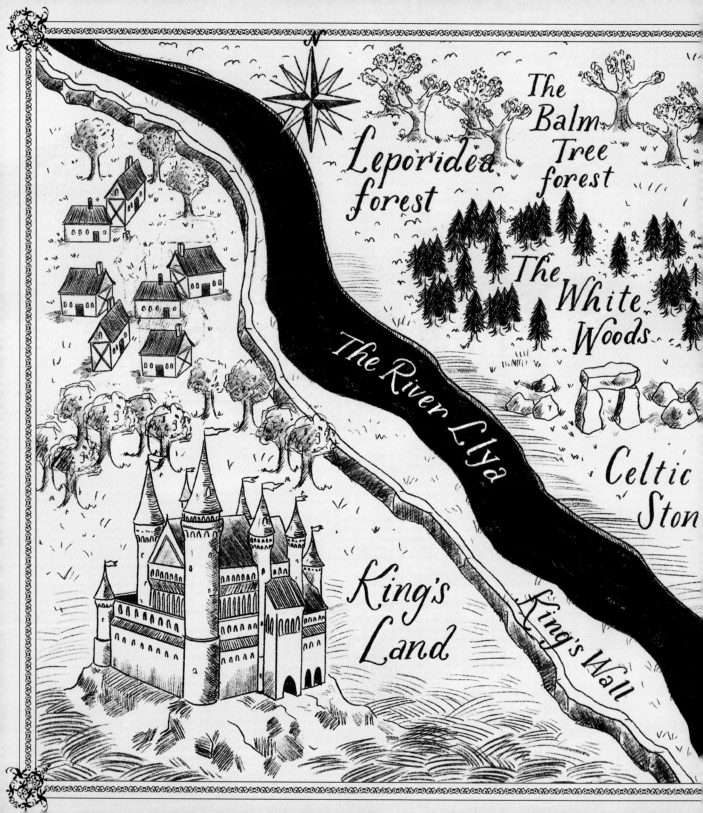

WHERE THE BALM TREES GROW

In a faraway land called Girard, the **majestic harvest moon** shone brightly upon the **Leporidae** forest. Ou rabbit warren is in ancient woods, and many forest animals live upon us peacefully.

On this day, Pa rabbit was out **foraging** for bark and conifer needles while Ma was nesting and preparing for her **kits** to arrive. She was about to give birth to my new brothers and sisters.

The wise old owl sat perched high above in the oldest **balm** tree as he always did right before new life was brought into the forest.

Day turned into night, and then day again. At the first signs of dawn, I saw Pa pop his head out of our **modest** little **burrow** calling out for me.

"Josie! Josieeee! It's time, they are here!" I flew down the **burrow** and saw Ma holding three baby bunnies; my sister Belle, my brother Jack, and my brother Silas.

Our hearts were so full they could burst.

It did not take long for the
bunnies to accompany Pa and I
out into the forest and do all
the things helpful bunnies did.
Once Ma finally agreed, we
allowed them to follow us
along the paths we had taken
one hundred times before. I
often turned around to check
on the bunnies and noticed
that one was missing.

It was Silas. He could not keep up, he was not hopping like his brother and sister were. Perhaps he hurt himself on a **brickleberry thorn**? I stopped to look. No, it wasn't a thorn. I looked down closely upon his hind legs. Our legs were unalike. It seemed Silas was different from the other little bunnies.

As soon as we returned to our home, Pa sent for the physician, Doctor Tod.
Ma said he was a healer, and for my sweet Silas, I wished it true.

Doctor Tod meticulously looked over Silas.

Nodding his head, he quickly closed his bag of medicinal tools, **elixirs**, and **salves**. He nodded again at my parents, and I saw him out. I could hear Ma and Pa talking softly by the light of the fire.

Pa just
embraced
Ma till she stopped crying.
I heard him say, "Yes, he is not like the
others, but he is more special through and
through. You will see my dear, you will see."

It was not easy for a bunny like Silas to exist in the forest without hopping and jumping. There was work, **foraging**, and chores to do. We worried about him.

Luckily, Silas had help from our friends; the wise old owl Ophelos, the majestic stag Gabriel, the brave bear Barnabas, and the clever twin squirrels Geminina and Coco.

Together, we protected Silas. We were more like family than friends.

At times, I was angry with the forest; after all, this is where the **balm** trees grow. Animals and even man would travel far and wide from other kingdoms and valleys, even mountain peaks, to seek out the magical **balm**. It healed the ill and all sickness. This wasn't the case for my Silas. Whatever could I do to help him be like the other bunnies?

When I was a tiny baby, Pa would tell me stories of the Fairy Queen, and how she would grant one wish to those most deserving—those with the purest of hearts.

But The Fairy Queen was far away in the Valley of the **Centaurs**, and I couldn't go alone. I asked the others to travel on this quest with me, surely for Silas they would.

We would have to travel on the night of the **winter solstice** and follow **the North Star**. The very next night, we set off into the wilderness.

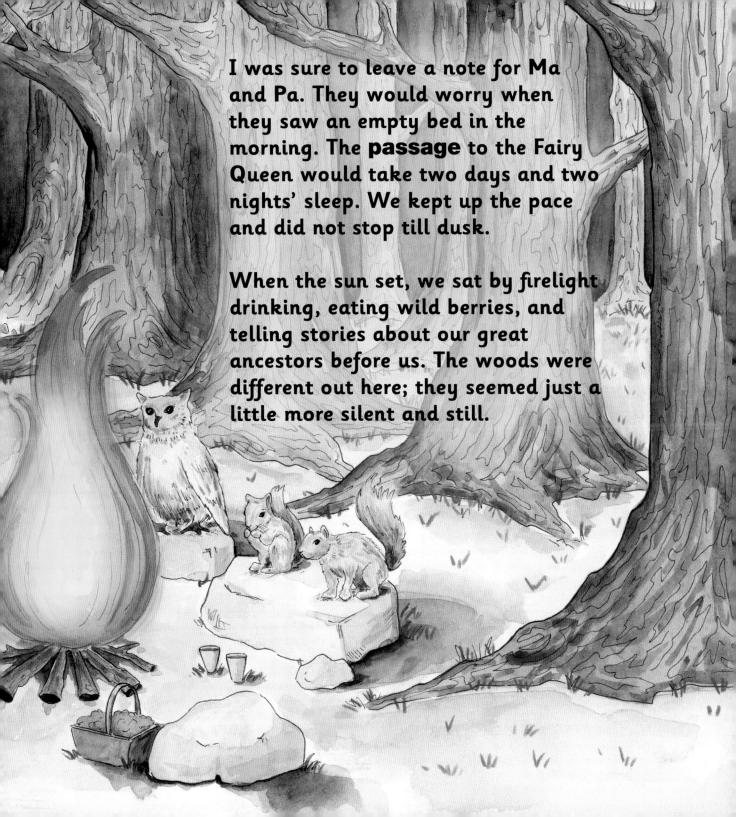

I was sure to leave a note for Ma and Pa. They would worry when they saw an empty bed in the morning. The **passage** to the Fairy Queen would take two days and two nights' sleep. We kept up the pace and did not stop till dusk.

When the sun set, we sat by firelight drinking, eating wild berries, and telling stories about our great ancestors before us. The woods were different out here; they seemed just a little more silent and still.

I never ventured this far out past the **Leoporidae** forest. The woodlands stretched far past the **horizon**. You could see the peaks of the highest mountain tops. I knew we were getting closer.

The Fairy Queen was just over the last summit into the Valley of the **Centaurs**. **The North Star** acted as our compass; the closer we got to Her Highness, the brighter it shined.

As soon as we touched down at the base of the mountain, we were greeted by two great **centaurs**.

"Her Highness is expecting you." They bowed and set off into the woods. We followed closely behind over a stream and through a door into a secret garden. This land was beautiful and mystical, I could feel her presence. Surely the Fairy Queen would grant us our wish of making Silas like all the other bunnies.

The Fairy Queen sat upon a magnificent throne of flowers. She spoke as soon as we entered. "Come closer, my dear. I have been following you throughout your journey, although you did not need much guidance. I am ready to hear your wish."

I spoke as loud as my little voice could go. "Your Highness, I have come all this way with my friends to ask you to please heal my brother, Silas. You see, he is different, not like the others. Surely it is best he is like the rest of us."

The Fairy Queen rose, "My sweet Josie, has Silas asked to be like everyone else?"

My friends and I all looked around at one another. I was not confident in my answer, "No, Your Highness, he has not."

"I can not grant you this wish. Silas is not different. He is more special in his own image—perfect and strong in ways you can not see." This never occurred to me and my friends before.

The Beautiful Fairy spoke again, "This journey that you all set out on for your dear friend has been a very important lesson learned.

"You will all leave here today, return to **Leoporidae**, and love one another exactly as you are. Spread this message of love and acceptance, it is your duty." We graciously accepted.

It occurred to me it was us that needed the help all along. We learned that everyone has their purpose in life and Silas had his, in time more would be revealed.

Ophelos, Gabriel, Barnabas, Geminina, Coco, and I were homeward bound. We missed our family and friends, especially Silas. We did not speak much on the long journey home, it gave us time to think about all the things we had to be grateful for. Before we knew it, we had entered **Leporidae** forest. I could see our home in the distance with smoke **billowing** out of our chimney, the familiar smell warmed my heart.

I could see Silas playing outside in the sun with Ma and Pa as he always did. I hopped as quickly as I could to Silas, hugged him tighter than ever before, and said, "Please do not ever ever change, I love you just the way you are."

Silas looked up at me and smiled. It felt good to be home—perfect just the way we are, every one of us.

THE END

GLOSSARY

MAJESTIC- HAVING OR SHOWING IMPRESSIVE BEAUTY OR DIGNITY.

HARVEST MOON- A FULL, BRIGHT MOON THAT OCCURS CLOSEST TO THE START OF AUTUMN. THE NAME DATES FROM THE TIME WHEN FARMERS DEPENDED ON THE MOON'S LIGHT TO HARVEST THEIR CROPS LATE INTO THE NIGHT.

LEPORIDAE- IS THE FAMILY OF RABBITS AND HARES, THE LATIN WORD LEPORIDAE MEANS "THOSE THAT RESEMBLE LEPUS" (HARE).

FORAGING- OBTAIN FOOD OR PROVISIONS FROM (A PLACE).

KITS- A BABY RABBIT IS CALLED A KIT. KITS IS SHORT FOR KITTENS.

MODEST- LIMITED, OR SMALL.

BURROW- A HOLE OR TUNNEL DUG BY A SMALL ANIMAL, ESPECIALLY A RABBIT, AS A DWELLING.

BRICKLEBERRY THORN- A WOODY PLANT BEARING SHARP PRICKLES.

METICULOUSLY- EXTRA CARE IN THE CONSIDERATION OR TREATMENT OF DETAILS.

ELIXIRS- A MAGICAL OR MEDICINAL POTION.

SALVES- AN OINTMENT USED TO PROMOTE HEALING OF THE SKIN OR AS PROTECTION.

BALM- A TREE THAT YIELDS A FRAGRANT STICKY SUBSTANCE, ESPECIALLY ONE USED IN MEDICINE.

CENTAUR- A CREATURE FROM GREEK MYTHOLOGY THAT WAS HALF-MAN AND HALF-HORSE. THE HEAD, ARMS, AND TORSO WERE HUMAN AND JOINED AT THE WAIST TO THE BODY AND LEGS OF A HORSE.

WINTER SOLSTICE- THE SOLSTICE THAT MARKS THE ONSET OF WINTER AT THE TIME OF THE SHORTEST DAY AND THE LONGEST NIGHT OF THE YEAR. THE WINTER SOLSTICE HAS BEEN CELEBRATED IN SOME FORM ALL AROUND THE WORLD. THIS CAN OFTEN BE SEEN IN THE FOLKTALES FROM OTHER PARTS OF THE WORLD.

THE NORTH STAR- A BRIGHT STAR THAT CAN BE SEEN IN THE SKY IN NORTHERN PARTS OF THE WORLD WHEN ONE IS LOOKING DIRECTLY TOWARD THE NORTH.

PASSAGE- MOVING THROUGH, UNDER, OVER, OR PAST SOMETHING ON THE WAY FROM ONE PLACE TO ANOTHER.

HORIZON- WHERE THE SKY SEEMS TO MEET THE LAND.

BILLOWING- SMOKE, CLOUD, OR STEAM MOVING OR FLOWING OUTWARD.

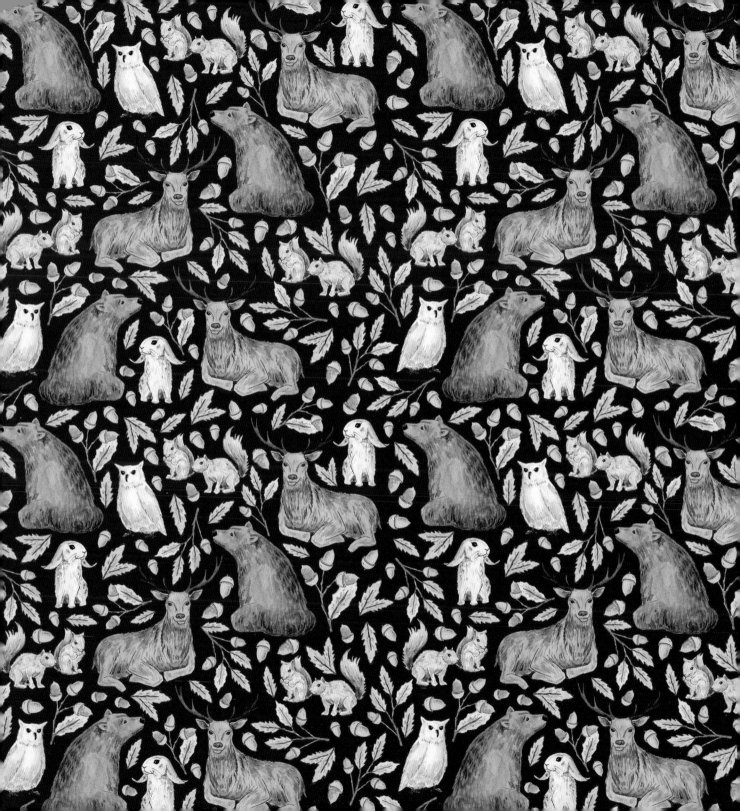